PIPER GREEN *and the* FAIRY TREE

GOING PLACES

Book

PIPER GREEN
and the
FAIRY TREE

GOING PLACES

ELLEN POTTER *Illustrated by* QIN LENG

Alfred A. Knopf | Yearling
New York

Text copyright © 2017 by Ellen Potter
Jacket art and interior illustrations copyright © 2017 by Qin Leng

All rights reserved. Published in the United States by
Alfred A. Knopf and Yearling, imprints of Random House Children's Books,
a division of Penguin Random House LLC, New York.

Knopf, Borzoi Books, and the colophon are registered
trademarks of Penguin Random House LLC.

Yearling and the jumping horse design are registered trademarks
of Penguin Random House LLC.

Visit us on the Web! randomhousekids.com

Educators and librarians, for a variety of teaching tools,
visit us at RHTeachersLibrarians.com

Library of Congress Cataloging-in-Publication Data
Names: Potter, Ellen, author. | Leng, Qin, illustrator.
Title: Going places / Ellen Potter ; illustrated by Qin Leng.
Description: First edition. | New York : Alfred A. Knopf, [2017] | Series: Piper Green and the
Fairy Tree ; book 4
Summary: Hidden in the fairy hole of the red maple tree are x-ray vision glasses that Piper takes
to school to use as her class learns about traveling to China.
Identifiers: LCCN 2016001076 (print) | LCCN 2016026348 (ebook) |
ISBN 978-1-101-93962-8 (lib. bdg.) | ISBN 978-1-101-93964-2 (pbk.) |
ISBN 978-1-101-93963-5 (ebook)
Subjects: | CYAC: Travel—Fiction. | Schools—Fiction. | Islands—Fiction.
Classification: LCC PZ7.P8518 Go 2017 (print) | LCC PZ7.P8518 (ebook) | DDC [Fic]—dc23

The text of this book is set in 17-point Mrs Eaves.
The illustrations were created using ink and digital painting.

Printed in the United States of America
January 2017
10 9 8 7 6 5 4 3 2 1

First Edition

First Yearling Edition 2017

For the students and staff at the Adams School.
You always bring sunshine into my day.
—E.P.

To Grandpa and Grandma
—Q.L.

Lighthouse

Piper's House

Fairy Tree

Ferry Landing

The Little Store

Peek-a-Boo ISLAND

Wharf

Woods

Double Cove

Peeka-Boo Island Harbor

Post Office

Library

Health Clinic

Fire Station

Tom Thumb Island

Goose Pond

Turtle Cove

Blueberry Cove

Granite Quarry

Cubbyhole Cove

Seal Ledge

Twin Sister Islands

CHAPTER
ONE

THE IMPORTANT STUFF

My name is Piper Green, and I live on Peek-a-Boo Island.

There are two things you should know about Peek-a-Boo Island:

1. All the kids on the island ride
   a lobster boat to school.

2. There is a Fairy Tree
   in my front yard.

If you don't like fairies or lobster boats, you can go do something else. For instance, you could make a belly-button garden. I made one last week. First I put some dirt in my little brother Leo's belly button. Then I watered the dirt and stuck a tomato seed in it. After that, I told Leo to lie outside in the sunshine so I could watch the seed sprout. Too bad Mom came along right at that moment.

"Leo, wash that dirt out of your belly button," she said. "Why would you let Piper talk you into doing such a crazy thing?"

"Because I like tomatoes," he told her.

CHAPTER TWO

MRS. SNORTINGHAM

When I got home from school, Mrs. Snortingham was relaxing on our living room floor. Her legs were sticking straight out, and she was snoring.

Mrs. Snortingham is a pig by the way.

Her owner, Nora Bean, was sitting on the couch with Mom.

"What's the matter with Mrs. Snortingham?" I asked.

When there is a strange animal in our living room, it usually means that it's not feeling well. Since there is no veterinarian on Peek-a-Boo Island, people take their sick animals to Mom because she is a nurse.

"Well," said Nora Bean, "the silly pig was in my kitchen this morning, watching me make her breakfast. I guess she was too hungry to wait because look what she tried to eat!" Nora Bean pointed to a flat, slimy-looking thing that was sitting on a towel on our coffee table. "Luckily your mom was able to get it out of her throat."

"What is it?" I asked.

"A refrigerator magnet," said Nora Bean.

"*Ooooh,* it's a little flip-flop!" said Leo, and he picked it up.

He is pretty disgusting at times.

"Can I have it?" he asked.

"You want something that we just pulled out of a *pig's mouth*?" Mom said.

"It's not for me," he answered.

He ran to his room. In a minute, he came back holding Michelle. She is a piece of paper. Leo says she is his wife.

"Michelle's been feeling kind of tired lately. I think she needs to get off her feet."

He wiped the pig slobber off the magnet with his shirt. Then he stuck Michelle on the fridge with the magnet.

She did look a little perkier that way actually.

Nora Bean reached into her pocket. She pulled out another refrigerator magnet. It was a tiny skateboard.

"If you want this one, Piper, you can have it," Nora Bean said. "Don't worry, there's no pig spit on it. Mrs. Snortingham knocked it off the fridge with her snout. She broke off the magnet, but you can use the skateboard as a toy."

I took the little skateboard. The wheels spun around and everything. If you were a teeny-tiny person, you could ride on it!

Suddenly, I had a brainchild. That's when a good idea pops out of your brain.

"Thanks, Nora Bean!" I said, and darted outside. I ran through our yard until I reached the fat red maple tree. That's the Fairy Tree. When you climb up to the first crook in the tree, you see a big hole in the trunk. If you put a treasure inside that hole, the fairies will take it, and they will leave you a new treasure in its place.

I climbed up the tree and balanced myself on the branch. Then I stuck my face next to the hole in the tree trunk.

"Hellooo in there," I said. "I have something that I think you guys are really going to like!"

I put the tiny skateboard inside the hole.

"Oh, wait a sec," I said. "I just remembered something."

I quick scrambled down the tree. I looked around the yard until I found half a walnut shell. Then I climbed back up the Fairy Tree again.

"You can use this as a helmet so you're not against the law." I put the walnut shell inside the hole too.

I started to climb down, but then I climbed back up again. "And just in case you need some ideas of what to leave for me . . . an invisible-ink pen would be good. Oh, and those secret-agent night-vision goggles I asked for a while ago? FYI, they would still come in handy."

CHAPTER THREE

BONES

In the morning, before school, I went outside to see if the fairies had left me anything. I climbed up the Fairy Tree, reached inside the hole, and felt around.

There *was* something in there! When I pulled it out and looked at it, my face became shocked. They were secret-agent night-vision glasses! That was very surprising because those fairy people never leave me anything I ask for.

"Thank you, thank you!" I yelled into the fairy hole. "I love them!"

"Good morning, Piper."

I looked down to see our neighbor Mrs. Pennypocket and her bull terrier, Nigel, staring up at me.

"Hi, Mrs. Pennypocket. Guess what? You know how you always say that the Fairy Tree gives you stuff that you need, instead of stuff that you want? Well, this time they left me something that I really wanted! Secret-agent night-vision glasses!" I reached down and handed her the glasses. They had red swirlies on each lens and thick black plastic rims.

"Oooh, very nice, Piper, very nice," Mrs. Pennypocket said while she looked them over. "Except for one thing. These aren't secret-agent night-vision glasses."

"They aren't?"

"No. They're X-ray vision glasses. Come on down here, and I'll show you how they work."

I climbed down, and Mrs. Pennypocket handed me the glasses.

"Put these on, Piper."

I put on the glasses.

"Now look at my hand," said Mrs. Pennypocket.

She held up her hand and I looked at it.

"Oh!" I said. "Everything looks all funny. Whoa, I think I can see your *bones,* Mrs. Pennypocket!!"

I lifted the glasses off my nose, then put them on again. "Yup, there they are. They

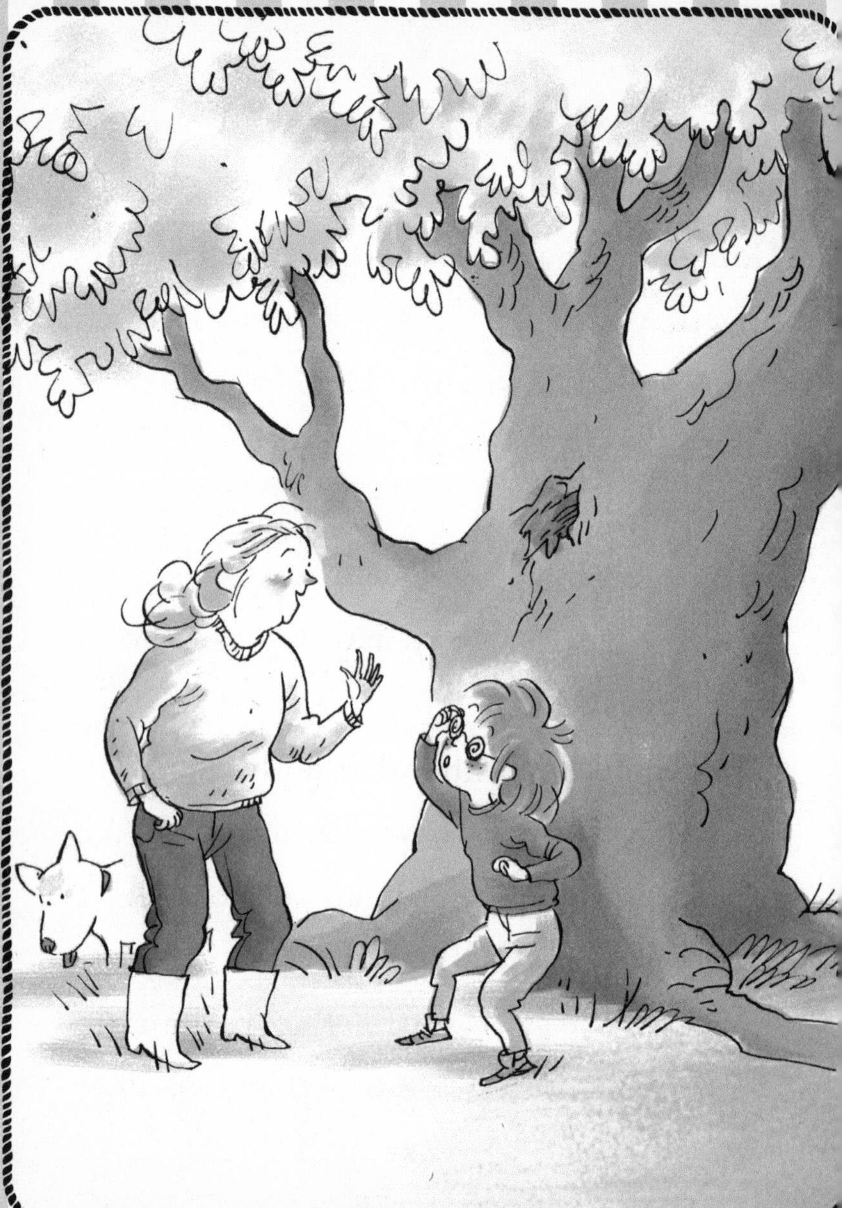

look pretty starving. Maybe you should eat a little more."

Mrs. Pennypocket laughed. "You have fun with those, Piper," she said, and walked off with Nigel.

～～

"Nice glasses, Piper," said Mr. Grindle as Leo and I boarded the *Maddie Rose* that morning.

Mr. Grindle owns the *Maddie Rose,* which is the lobster boat that takes us to our school on Mink Island each day.

"Thanks," I said. "They're X-ray. I can see inside of you, Mr. Grindle."

"Can you? How do things look in there?" he asked.

"Pretty good." I gave him the thumbs-up.

I went into the wheelhouse to see what Mrs. Grindle had put in her basket today. Every day, Mrs. Grindle bakes a treat for all the kids who go to school on the *Maddie Rose.* Today there were thick slices of pumpkin bread. I took a piece and went out onto the deck to see my friend Jacob. He was already there, munching on his pumpkin bread.

"Don't be embarrassed," I told him.

"Why should I be?" he asked.

"Because I can see under your shirt with these glasses," I told him. "But I can only see your bones, so it's okay. Here." I handed the glasses to Jacob. "You can X-ray *me*."

Jacob put them on and looked through them for a second. Then he took them off and gave them back to me.

"It's some kind of trick," Jacob said.

"How can it be a trick? You can see bones, Jacob. Actual *bones*!"

Jacob just shrugged and took another bite of pumpkin bread.

That boy can be very aggravating.

CHAPTER
FOUR

X-RAY X-PERT

I sat in the classroom before school began, thinking of all the things I could do with X-ray vision. Like I could open an X-ray stand. It would be sort of like a lemonade stand. I could call it X-Ray X-Pert, and for fifty cents, I could tell people if they had any broken bones in their body.

Another thing I could do was see through walls to spy on people.

I put on the glasses and stared at the wall. Then I remembered that the bathroom is on the other side of the wall, and

I did *not* want to see anything going on in that place. So instead, I stared at Camilla, the girl who sits next to me.

"Those glasses are *so* funny," Camilla said.

I just kept looking at her.

"Why are you looking at me like that?" Camilla asked.

"I'm trying to see your brain," I told her.

"Oh, that reminds me. I'm going to be a bottle of hot sauce for Halloween this year."

"What does that have to do with me seeing your brain?" I asked.

"Because my brain thought of it," she said.

Just then, our teacher Ms. Arabella swished into our class. She always wears swishy dresses, and she has swishy blond princess hair. The rest of her is all business, you'd better believe it, buster.

I decided to try out my X-ray vision on Ms. Arabella's brain. I stared at her head very watchfully while she put her giant tote bag on her desk.

"Good morning, everyone," she said, smiling. When she saw me, though, her face stopped smiling.

"Piper, please take off those glasses."

So I had to take them off before I could see her brain.

Allie O'Malley raised her hand.

"What's in your tote bag, Ms. Arabella?" asked Allie.

Usually, the only thing Ms. Arabella carries in her tote bag is more work for us and her lunch. But today it had a big, round bump in it.

"Actually, I do have something special in my bag today," said Ms. Arabella. "You have sharp eyes, Allie!"

Allie looked around at everyone to make sure we had all heard what Ms. Arabella said. That made me feel grumpy because if Ms. Arabella hadn't made me take off my glasses, I might have seen her brains, and eyes don't get any sharper than that.

"Does anyone have any guesses as to what's in my tote bag?" asked Ms. Arabella.

Hunter's hand shot up. He always raises his hand even if he has no idea what he's talking about.

"Is it a ghost?" Hunter said.

I bet if I used my X-ray vision on Hunter's head, all I'd see inside there would be a bunch of fluff balls.

CHAPTER
FIVE

BUNNY-EAR FINGERS

Ms. Arabella reached into her tote bag. She pulled out a spinning globe on a little metal stand and put it on her desk. The countries on the globe were all different colors and were bumpy.

"This week, our class is going to travel around the world," she said. When she said the word "travel," she held up two fingers on both hands, like bunny ears, and then she curled down the tips of those fingers. Bunny-ear fingers mean that what you are saying isn't exactly true. I know this because whenever Mom says that she'll take the one o'clock ferry, she makes bunny-ear fingers around "one o'clock," since the ferry never actually leaves on time.

"Each day, we'll visit a different country and learn all about it. Our first destination will be China."

"*Oooh!* My mom was born in China!" my best friend, Ruby, said. "And I've been there three times to visit my great-grandma."

"Ruby, can you come up and show us where China is on the globe?" Ms. Arabella asked.

Ruby jumped out of her seat and went up to the globe. She spun it around and then put her finger on a big purple bump that was shaped like a chicken.

"Very good, Ruby!" said Ms. Arabella as Ruby sat back down.

Ms. Arabella reached into the tote bag again. This time she pulled out a hat. It was dark blue with a big, shiny brim. Above the brim was a gold band, and above the band were golden wings. She put the hat on her head. She looked very cute.

"This week, I'll be Captain Arabella," Ms. Arabella said, "because we will be traveling by plane and I will be your pi-lot." She made those bunny-ear fingers again when she said the word "pilot."

"Aye, aye, Captain," I heard Jacob whisper. I looked over at him. His eyes were all lovey because Ms. Arabella looked so cute in her hat.

That made me *harrumph.* Just in my head, though.

Allie O'Malley raised her hand.

"I've been on a plane *six* times," said Allie. "And once, they lost our suitcases and we had to buy socks and underwear in a drugstore."

Then everyone got all excited, and they started shouting out *their* plane stories.

"I went on a plane to South Carolina, and they gave us little bags of pretzels," said Nicole.

"I once went on a plane to Chicago," Jacob said.

I was shocked at that news because I know everything about Jacob and he never said anything about being on a plane!

I didn't have an airplane story. That's because I've never been on one. NEVER. The farthest away I've ever been is to my aunt Terry's spa, which only takes fifteen minutes by boat.

"When we went on a plane, I barfed," said Garth. That wasn't surprising because there is always something gross coming out of Garth's mouth, although usually it is a giant belch that smells like Cheerios. "Good thing they had barf bags on the plane!"

Ms. Arabella picked up her bottle marked "Quiet Spray" and sprayed it into the air a few times. No one knows what's in Quiet Spray. Ruby says she thinks it's just water, but it does make us all stop yabbering.

"Okay, class, raise your hand if you've been on a plane before," said Ms. Arabella.

And guess what? Everyone raised their hand. EVERYONE!! Even fluff-brain Hunter.

So the only thing I could do was raise my hand too.

"Wow, I see I have a classroom of experienced flyers! That's wonderful! And since Allie and Piper were the only ones

who remembered to raise their hands before they spoke, they will have special jobs. Allie will be in charge of security. Piper, you will be our flight attendant."

"Yay!" I said, trying to sound excited.

But I should have made bunny-ear fingers for my "yay" because I had no idea what a flight attendant does.

CHAPTER SIX

BRAIN POPCORN

Ms. Arabella gave us each an empty cereal box to make into a suitcase for our trip. On my cereal box was a picture of a smiling shark eating a bowl of cereal using his fins. It was the kind of cereal with little bright blue crunch balls, which I'm not allowed to eat because Mom says that no food should be blue, except for blueberries. The box smelled delicious, though.

I glued green paper on my cereal-box suitcase and drew squiggles all over it. After that, I looked for things to put inside

it. First I put in my X-ray glasses. I looked in my backpack for more stuff, but there wasn't anything good in there. Except I did find a dried-up piece of chewed gum that was sort of in the shape of an egg roll, which is my favorite Chinese food, so I put that in the suitcase too.

While we decorated, Ms. Arabella went around and took pictures of us. For my picture, I tried to smile like the blue crunch-ball shark.

By the time we finished decorating our cereal-box suitcases, we had to leave for gym class. We were doing flexibility this week, so Ruby, Camilla, Allie, and I all sat on the gym floor together and stretched ourselves.

"I can't wait for our trip today!" Ruby said. "I love planes. Well, I don't like it when they're bouncy. My favorite part is when we're in the clouds."

"For spring break, my family and I are flying to Florida," said Allie. "For the *third* time."

"One time we went to New York City," said Camilla, "and we saw a mermaid parade. We also saw a guy wearing a hat made of socks getting arrested."

I felt jealous just listening to all those great places everyone had been. I would LOVE to see a mermaid parade and watch a guy in a sock hat getting arrested!

But all I've ever seen is nothing.

"You never told me you'd been on a plane before, Piper," Ruby said. "Where did you go?"

"Oh, all over the place," I told her. I worried if my face was looking funny because I was lying, so I pretended I had an itch on my forehead. I scratched it so that my face could duck behind my hand.

"Really?" Allie said. "Like *where*?" She said it in that voice of hers that I hate. It's the voice that acts as if it knows something bad about you.

"Like Africa," I said. I thought for a second and scratched my forehead some more. "And that place with the Heightful Tower. Utah, it's called."

After that, the lies just started popping out my mouth. It was like when you make popcorn in a pan and you use too many kernels and they start flying all over the place. *Pop, pop, pop!* I just couldn't stop them!

"I've gone to all those places because my uncle is a pilot," I said. "His name is Uncle Bobby." *Pop, pop, pop!* "And he flies people all over the world." *Pop, pop, pop!* "Sometimes he lets me sit up front with him and drive the plane. It's not as hard as you would think." *Pop, pop, pop, pop!!!*

"Wow! Do you think he'd let me fly his plane sometime, Piper?" Ruby asked.

"Yup," I said. My forehead was starting to itch for real.

"You're so lucky that Ms. Arabella made you flight attendant," said Camilla. "You'll get to give out snacks and barf bags. Plus, you get to say the 'in case of an emergency' speech."

I had a lumpy feeling in my stomach because I didn't want to give out barf bags and I didn't know what speech she was talking about.

CHAPTER
SEVEN

SUPER SNOOPER

When we went back to our classroom, the door was closed. Ms. Arabella was standing in the hallway, wearing her blue captain's hat. She held a big manila envelope.

"Hello, passengers! My name is Captain Arabella." She took a bunch of blue booklets out of her envelope. "These are your passports," she said as she handed them out. "Keep them in your suitcases. When we get to each country, I'll stamp your passport. That proves you have visited that country."

I opened my passport. A photo of me was glued onto the first page. I was smiling like the blue crunch-ball shark.

It wasn't my best picture.

"All right." Captain Arabella looked at us and clapped her hands. "Let's start our journey."

She opened the door and OH WOW! Because there was a plane right in the middle of our classroom!

All our desks were gone, and our chairs were set up in two rows. There were also two chairs in the front of the plane, one behind the other. Long pieces of cardboard were taped together and wrapped all around the outside of our chairs. The cardboard was painted white with a red stripe down the center. It had little round windows cut into it and airplane wings coming out the sides and everything! The words "Island Airlines" were painted along the side too.

Of course we all rushed over to the plane, but Captain Arabella told us we couldn't board just yet.

"First everyone has to go through security." Captain Arabella pointed to her desk. On top of it was a long cardboard box, painted black, which was open at two ends. Next to it was a clear plastic bin. All our cereal-box suitcases were lined up on her desk too.

From her tote bag, Captain Arabella pulled out a little pin in the shape of an airplane. She pinned it on Allie O'Malley's shirt.

"Allie, you'll be running the luggage scanner," she said.

"What's a luggage scanner?" I asked Ruby.

She gave me a funny look. "A *luggage scanner*, Piper. *You* know."

"It X-rays your suitcase to make sure no one smuggles anything on the plane," Jacob said.

"Ohhh, right," I mumbled. "I forgot about those scanner things."

Then I had another brainchild! I already had X-ray glasses! I should be the one in charge of security, and Allie could be in charge of barf bags and that speech.

"Captain Arabella!" I rushed over to her and Allie. "Allie and I should trade jobs because look." I reached into my suitcase and pulled out my X-ray glasses. "I can put on my glasses and just stare at the suitcases to see what's inside them. I'm like a super snooper when I wear these. I'm perfect for the job."

"Piper, you're the flight attendant; Allie is security. Now please get in line with everyone else, and Allie will scan your luggage."

I wasn't happy about it, but I got in line

behind Camilla. Garth was the first person to have his suitcase scanned. He put his suitcase into the plastic bin and put the bin in the big black box. Allie reached in through the other side of the box and slid the bin out.

"BEEP, BEEP, BEEP!" said Allie. "I'll have to look inside your suitcase, sir." She was very professional. You could tell she had been to lots of airports.

She turned Garth's suitcase upside down.

Something fell out of it.

Allie looked at it.

Everyone else looked at it too. It was small and reddish and splotchy-shaped.

"What is that thing?" Allie asked Garth.

"A piece of my face," he told her.

Then he pointed to a white splotchy-shape of skin on his forehead where a scab used to be.

Blech.

Next was Nicole's suitcase. Allie *beep*ed that one too. Nicole had packed a lot of stuff, so it took Allie a long time to go through it all. That was a good thing, I thought. Maybe if she took long enough, there wouldn't be time for my speech.

Next up was Camilla. She put her suitcase in the bin, and then she put the bin in the scanner. Allie pulled it out through the other side.

"Okay, your suitcase looks good, ma'am," Allie said.

"But you didn't even look in it!" I said to Allie. "She might have a stuffed animal or something inside it."

"So?" Allie said.

"So that's not allowed."

Allie put her hands on her hips. "What's wrong with bringing a stuffed animal, Piper?"

"There is no snuggling allowed on the plane, don't you know?" I said.

"Smuggling," I heard Jacob say very, very quietly behind my ear.

I got hot in my face.

Allie squinched up her eyes at me suspiciously.

"I said, no smuggling allowed," I mumbled.

"I am not smuggling!" Camilla said.

"Settle down, everyone!" said Captain Arabella. "No one is smuggling anything."

"But how can you be sure?" I said.

"Because you all have honest faces. So let's put the rest of the suitcases through the scanner, and we can all board the plane."

I put my suitcase in the bin, but I tried not to let Captain Arabella see my face. Because it was not being honest today.

CHAPTER EIGHT

IN CASE OF
EMERGENCY

When all our suitcases were scanned, Captain Arabella pulled another little airplane pin out of her bag. She pinned it on my shirt.

"Piper, you are officially a flight attendant," she said. "That's your seat up front, behind mine. After you put your suitcase under your chair, please make sure the passengers' suitcases are under their chairs too. I'm going to go check on something in the lunchroom. I'll be back in a minute."

I put my suitcase under my chair. Then I made sure that everyone else had their suitcases under their chairs too.

Everybody was chittering and chattering with excitement, except for me because I was too worried.

"Shhh, you guys!" Ruby said to everyone. "Now Piper is going to do the 'in case of emergency' speech."

She sat up straight and smiled at me. You could see that she was going to listen very carefully. Everyone got quiet and looked at me too.

Uh-oh.

I tried to think of all the things that I knew about emergencies. I suddenly remembered the firefighter who came to talk to our school last year. She gave us a coloring page of a fire truck and then told us what to do if a fire happens.

"In case your head goes on fire," I said, "just roll around on the floor till the fire goes out."

Everyone looked at me kind of confused. Jacob was doing little shakes of his head at me. I guessed I was supposed to say something more.

Then I remembered a commercial that always comes on when my dad watches the TV weather report. I remembered the whole thing perfectly, too, because it's on every single night.

"If you are injured in an accident, call the law offices of Sam Klammer and Sons," I said. "Your problem is our business."

I bowed quickly.

"The end," I said, and sat down.

"That is not what flight attendants say," Allie announced. "Have you *really* been on a plane, Piper? I mean, *ever*?"

Ruby leaned forward. "That was weird, Piper." Her voice sounded sort of nervous.

I felt my face get hot again.

Luckily, Captain Arabella came back right then. She sat down in the chair at the front of the plane. She was holding a joystick from a video game in her lap.

"Good morning, folks. This is your captain speaking." She put her hand over her mouth so that her voice made a muffled sound. "You are flying on Island Airlines, destined for Beijing, China's capital city. The weather in Beijing is sixty-five degrees, with plenty of sunshine. On Island Airlines, we take safety very seriously, so please buckle your seat belts."

We all pretended to buckle our seat belts.

Captain Arabella took hold of the joystick. She made an engine sound with her mouth. She did a good job. It got louder and louder and louder.

"Prepare for takeoff!" she said.

Captain Arabella's head leaned back, as if the plane was going up in the air. All of us leaned our heads back too.

After a minute, Captain Arabella announced, "We have now reached our cruising altitude of thirty-five thousand feet. You can unbuckle your seat belts. Sit back, relax, and enjoy the flight." She sat up straight again. Everybody else did too.

"I can see clouds!" said Camilla, looking out the round windows.

"I see mountains down below!" said Garth.

Suddenly, I had an idea.

I began to bounce in my seat.

That's because I remembered what Ruby said about how the plane was bouncy.

"What are you doing?" Jacob asked.

"Riding in a plane," I said.

I bounced a little faster.

"Piper, please stay in your seat," said Captain Arabella.

I sat back in my seat. After a minute, though, I made the seat rockity around.

Rockity, rockity, rockity.

ROCKITY, ROCKITY, ROCKITY!!

The kids started laughing.

"Piper." Captain Arabella turned and looked at me. "Stop that."

"Watch where you're going, Captain, or

we'll fly right into those mountains over there!" screeched Garth.

That made me rockity-rockity like mad!

All of a sudden, my chair slid out from under me. It flew up in the air, and I crashed down on the ground.

After that, Captain Arabella told me to take my suitcase and sit out in the hallway.

We had to make an emergency landing and everything.

CHAPTER
NINE

SPILLING MY BEANS

I sat on the floor in the hallway. I tried not to cry, but my heart felt too tragic. Not only was I the only person in my class who had never gone *any*where, but now I couldn't even go to bunny-ear-fingers China.

The news got even worse, though. My suitcase was totally smooshed because I landed on it when I fell off my chair. I stuck my hand inside it to check on my X-ray glasses. My fingers felt too many pieces of things in there. I pulled out one of those pieces, and guess what? It was part of my X-ray glasses, all smashed up.

I sat there and cried and cried until even my nose was leaking. When I heard the classroom door open, I quickly tried to wipe up my face with my shirt.

It was Jacob.

"Ms. Arabella says you can come back in now," he told me.

He handed me a whole wad of tissues.

"How did you know I was crying?" I asked. My voice sounded squeaky.

He shrugged.

I wiped up my face while Jacob waited. That's when I decided to spill my beans.

"Jacob?"

"What?"

"I've never been on a plane before," I told him.

"Yeah, I figured," he said.

"I've never gone anywhere in my whole entire life," I told him.

"You will, Piper," he said.

"*Hmmph,*" I said glumly.

"You might even go to the real China someday," Jacob said.

I snuffled back the leaks in my nose.

"Maybe when we're married?" I said.

Jacob sighed, then turned to go back into the classroom.

In the classroom, the plane had already landed. Everybody was standing in line by Captain Arabella's desk. They were holding their suitcases and their passports, and Captain Arabella was asking them questions and then stamping their passports.

I got in line behind Ruby. She looked at my eyeballs, which still felt wet and swollen.

"Are you okay?" she asked.

Now that I had already spilled my beans

once, it felt a little easier to spill them again.

"Ruby, I've never been on a plane before. Not even one time."

"You were lying?" said Ruby.

"Yes," I said. "I'm really sorry."

Ruby looked so disappointed that I couldn't even stand it. I stared down at my sneakers so I wouldn't have to see that sorrowful face.

"Does that mean your uncle Bobby isn't really a pilot either?" she asked.

"No," I said. "I got a little carried away there. I don't even have an uncle Bobby."

"Oh, shoot," she said. "I really wanted to drive his plane."

I had a solution for that problem, though.

"Hey, Ruby, when you grow up, you could become a pilot," I said. "And you could wear that cute hat and drive planes all over the place."

"Oh yeah. I could," said Ruby. "If I was a pilot, I could visit my great-grandma whenever I felt like it." She cheered right up, so I felt a little better about things too.

When I got to Captain Arabella's desk, she smiled at me in a nice way.

"May I see your passport please, miss?" Her hat was not on her head anymore.

"Are you still the pilot?" I asked.

"Nope. Now I am a customs agent," she said.

Good! I thought. Because it was the pilot who kicked me off the plane.

Ms. Arabella looked at my passport photo carefully. Then she looked up at my face, then down at the photo again.

"That really is me in the picture," I told her. "I was just smiling like the blue crunch-ball shark."

"Okay, Miss Green, you are all set," said Ms. Arabella. She stamped my passport. The stamp was of a panda bear. "Have a pleasant visit."

Once everyone was stamped, we followed Ms. Arabella down the hallway. She stopped in front of the lunchroom door.

"Are you ready for China?" she asked. She wiggled her eyebrows.

"YES!! YES!! YES!!" we screamed, and jumped around.

Ms. Arabella squinched up her face at that.

"Let's hope China is ready for you," she said quietly.

CHAPTER
TEN

NI HAO!

The lunchroom looked very festive! There were red paper lanterns hanging from the ceiling and posters of different places in China taped to the walls. There was a delicious smell coming from the kitchen too. And guess who was there? Ruby's mom, Mrs. Biggie! Only she wasn't dressed like Ruby's mom. She wore a beautiful shiny green dress with a funny high collar. Her black hair was in a bun, and she had little flowers all around the bun.

"Mom!" Ruby cried out. "You didn't tell me you were coming!"

"I wanted it to be a surprise," said Mrs. Biggie. She turned to all of us. *"Ni hao!"* It sounded like "knee how." "That means 'hello' in Chinese."

"Mrs. Biggie is going to tell you some interesting things about China," said Ms. Arabella.

Ms. Arabella had us all sit down at a round table. There was a lot of stuff on the table, like a soccer ball, drawing paper, a tiny, fuzzy white oval thing on a plate, a kite, a roll of toilet paper, red nail polish, and a compass.

"So many things!" said Mrs. Biggie.

"What do you think they all have in common?"

Hunter raised his hand.

"They're all on the same table," he said.

Mrs. Biggie laughed. "That's true, but they have something else in common too. They were all invented in China. The Chinese are great inventors."

"Especially if they invented toilet paper," said Garth. He opened his arms wide and yelled, "I love you, Chinese inventors!"

Ms. Arabella gave him the stink eye.

"What's that?" I asked, pointing to the tiny, fuzzy white oval thing in the dish.

"Ahh! Now that is something very

interesting." Mrs. Biggie carefully picked up the little white thing and held it out in the palm of her hand for us to see. "It's a cocoon made of silk. Inside this ball is a tiny worm called a silkworm. The silkworm makes the silk. Chinese people discovered how to use silk to create all kinds of beautiful things. My dress is made out of silk."

"But how does the worm make the silk? Worms don't have hands," I said.

"They spit it out," Mrs. Biggie said.

"Your dress is made of worm spit?"

"More or less," Mrs. Biggie said.

Then we all wanted to touch her worm-spit dress, so she let us.

"Can we see the worm?" asked Nicole.

"Nope. It's tucked safely inside its cocoon."

"I know how we can see it!" Camilla said. "We can use Piper's X-ray glasses!"

"No we can't," I said. "I sat on them. Look."

I turned my suitcase upside down and spilled everything out on the table.

I stared down at all the broken pieces. Then I frowned.

Because there was something in there that I definitely didn't pack!

CHAPTER
ELEVEN

GOING PLACES

"How did these get in there?" I said.

Two little white feathers had fallen out of my suitcase.

I picked them up and looked at them. They didn't belong to Yikes, our class parakeet. Yikes has lime-green and yellow feathers.

"May I see them, Piper?" Mrs. Biggie asked.

I gave her the feathers, and she held them up. Then she smiled.

"Those feathers were in your X-ray

glasses. My brother used to have a pair of those when he was a kid. Feathers are put between each lens, and it makes it look as if you're seeing bones."

"Do you mean I wasn't *really* seeing bones?" I asked.

"No. It's an optical illusion. That means it tricked your eyes into seeing something."

I sighed. "Mrs. Biggie, this has not been a good day for me."

"Not a good day?!" cried Mrs. Biggie. "Piper, don't you know what finding a feather means?"

I shook my head.

"Well, when I was a little girl, back in

China, I found a feather on my way home from school. A little white feather, just like this one. I showed it to my grandmother, and she said, 'Lucky you! When you find a feather, it means that you will fly off on a big trip very soon.' And she was right, because a few months later, my family took our first trip to America."

I thought about that. "What does *two* feathers mean?" I asked.

"Two feathers?" Mrs. Biggie smiled a big smile. "Two feathers mean that Piper Green is going places!"

CHAPTER TWELVE

CAT AND MOUSE

It turned out that the delicious smell was Chinese food called pot stickers, which Mrs. Biggie had made for us. They looked like fat little ears, and they were filled with chicken and vegetables. Mrs. Biggie showed us how to pick up the pot stickers with chopsticks and dip them in sauce. Ruby was the only one who could do it. The rest of us kept dropping the pot stickers on the floor. Then Garth shoved the chopsticks up his nose, which I knew he was going to do. Ms. Arabella's face started turning pink, and when it turns that color, you had better watch out.

"I think we should all just use our fingers to eat instead," said Ms. Arabella in her stern voice.

That worked out better.

After we ate, Mrs. Biggie showed us a very fun game that Chinese kids play called Cat and Mouse. Everyone held hands and made a circle. I was the cat, so I was outside the circle. Jacob was the mouse, so he was inside. The kids who were holding hands went round and round, to make the circle spin. When they stopped, I tried to catch Jacob by running in and out under everyone's hands. They were all screeching, "Run, Mouse, run! Run, Mouse, run!" But I caught Jacob on the second try.

"Got you!" I said, grabbing him around his waist.

Except it was really a hug, which is just my own secret.

When I got back home, I dropped off my backpack in the house and went straight outside to the Fairy Tree. I climbed up to the crook in the trunk and sat down.

"Hi, guys," I said to the hole in the tree. "I brought you a present. You don't have to leave me a present back either. This one is a freebie."

I took the white feathers out of my back pocket and carefully put one of them in the fairy hole.

"I thought you might need this since you probably get bored just living in a tree hole all the time. The feather means that you will go on a big trip someday. And see"—I held up the other feather—"I'm keeping one of the feathers too. So now all of us are going places. And after we go places, I think we should just come straight back to Peek-a-Boo Island, okay? That's the best plan because that's where everyone we know is."

I put my feather back in my pocket.

"Okay, you guys. Now I'm going to chew some gum into the shape of a pizza because guess where we are going tomorrow? Bunny-ear-fingers Italy!"

THE END

PIPER GREEN and the FAIRY TREE

PIE GIRL

POOF!

"Apple pie, pecan pie, butterscotch swirl,
Pumpkin pie, lumpkin pie,
I'm the pie GIRL!"

I made up that song this morning. I sang it as I walked to the Little Store with my younger brother, Leo. Every time I got to the part that went "GIRL," I did a hop.

"There's no such thing as lumpkin pie," said Leo.

Actually, I knew that. Except "lumpkin" was the only word that sounded good with "pumpkin."

I ignored him and sang my pie girl song again very loudly. I was in a joyful mood this morning, and I didn't want anything to ruin it. That's because today the *Sea Star* was coming. The *Sea Star* is a ship that sails around the coast of Maine, helping people who live on the islands. The *Sea Star*'s crew brings food when the weather is bad and people can't get across to the mainland, and at Christmas, they give all the kids presents. Plus, once a year, they bring doctors to the islands so that people can have checkups. Today they were coming with a doctor. But that's not the good part.

The good part was afterward, when there would be a potluck supper on board the ship. Everyone on the island brings food to the potluck supper, and whatever dish your family makes, the kids get to serve it.

This year, Mom was making pecan pie. That made me the Pie Girl.

The Little Store was very busy this morning. It is Peek-a-Boo Island's only grocery store, and it sells all kinds of things—bread, milk, cheese, ice cream, rubber gloves for lobstermen, and lots of other stuff too. Mrs. Spratt was behind the checkout counter. Her cash register kept going *Ping! Ping! Ping!* as people bought ingredients for their dish in the potluck supper.

I looked at our list:

> 2 bags of pecans
> 1 bag of brown sugar
> 1 bag of flour

Suddenly, I felt something *bonk* the back of my head.

"Hey!" I shouted as I turned around. Allie O'Malley was standing behind me, waving a wand with a silver glittery star on the end of it.

"What's the big idea?" I demanded, rubbing my head.

"I was poofing you," said Allie. She waved her wand around in the air. "Poof, poof! I'm being a fairy today. See? I'm wearing my brand-new fairy skirt." She twirled around to show off her skirt, which was made of green and silver cloth strips that were pointy on the bottom. It was very beautiful. Then she bonked Leo on the head with her wand.

"Poof!" she said.

"*OW!*" cried Leo.

"Fairies don't go around poofing people on their skulls, you know," I told her.

"Says who?" Allie O'Malley asked.

Right then I really felt like telling her about the Fairy Tree in my yard. Except I didn't because it's a secret. The only other person who knows about the Fairy Tree is my next-door neighbor Mrs. Pennypocket. There is a hole inside the Fairy Tree's trunk, and if you put something in there, the fairies will take it and leave you a special gift in its place.

I shut my mouth very tightly in case the Fairy Tree secret tried to sneak out of me.

"My mom is making a deviled eggs appetizer for the potluck," said Allie O'Malley as she swished her wand around. "So I'm going to be Appetizer Girl this year. Appetizer Girl is kind of like the star of the show because appetizers get served first."

"Well, I'm going to be Pie Girl," I said proudly.

Allie O'Malley frowned. "No you're not," she said. "You're Mashed Potato Girl. Your mother always makes mashed potatoes, so you are *always* Mashed Potato Girl."

"Well, guess what? This year, Mom isn't making mashed potatoes." I put my hand on my hip and bopped it to one side, very sassy.

"I liked it better when she made mashed potatoes," Leo said.

"That's because you were Gravy Boy," I told him.

Gravy Boy gets to pour the gravy from a little ceramic ship that is shaped like the *Titanic*. Mashed Potato Girl just plops the mashed potatoes on people's plates. No one wants to be a potato plopper.

"This year, our mom is making pecan pie," I said to Allie, shaking the bag of pecans at her, "so I'm going to be Pie Girl. *Pie Girl*."

I could tell that Allie was not happy about this news. Pie Girl is definitely better than Appetizer Girl because who doesn't love pie?

Mr. Aronson walked by with a shopping basket full of stuff. Allie screeched and jumped backward, squinching up her eyes.

"What's the matter?" asked Leo.

"Salt!" Allie shrieked, pointing to the container of salt in Mr. Aronson's basket.

"So? What's wrong with salt?" I asked.

"Fairies hate salt!"

"No they don't," I told her.

"Yes they do, Piper. They hate salt and they hate the sound of bells, and they love butterflies that are yellow and they love riding on giant rats."

"Says who?" I asked.

"My big fairy encyclopedia. It knows everything there is to know about fairies."

I felt a little sick in my stomach just then.

"They probably just don't like too *much* salt," I said with a nervous voice.

"Wrong!" Allie jabbed the wand at me. "Fairies hate any salt at all. My encyclopedia says that if you want to get rid of fairies, just sprinkle salt all around their house and they'll go away."

Uh-oh.

Because guess what I left for the fairies yesterday?

A pretzel rod. And that thing was covered with salt.

ABOUT THE AUTHOR

Although she doesn't ride a lobster boat to work, **Ellen Potter** can look out her window and see islands, just like the one Piper lives on. Ellen is the author of many books for children, including the award-winning Olivia Kidney series. She lives in Maine with her family and an assortment of badly behaved creatures. Learn more about Ellen at ellenpotter.com.

ABOUT THE ILLUSTRATOR

Qin Leng was born in Shanghai and lived in France and Montreal, where she studied at the Mel Hoppenheim School of Cinema. She has received many awards for her animated short films and artwork, and has published numerous picture books. Qin currently lives and works as a designer and illustrator in Toronto.